I AM READING

Sniffer and Naughty Nancy

ROGER ABBOTT

Illustrated by

KINGFISHER
An imprint of Kingfisher Publications Plc
New Penderel House, 283-288 High Holborn
London WC1V 7HZ
www.kingfisherpub.com

First published by Kingfisher 2006
2 4 6 8 10 9 7 5 3 1

A CIP catalogue record for this book
is available from the British Library.

ISBN-13: 978 0 7534 1319 7
ISBN-10: 0 7534 1319 1

Printed in China
1TR/0106/WKT/SCHOY/115MA/C

Contents

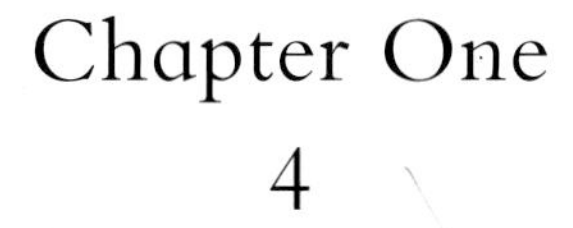

Chapter One

Nancy lived a naughty life deep in the forest in the land of Trittledore.

Nancy shared her tumbledown cottage with her pet dog named Sniffer.

Sniffer was a special dog, a bloodhound, who had a nose like a ripe, golden tomato.

Naughty Nancy loved all things that glittered. She had trained Sniffer to sniff out anything made of gold.

Every night, Nancy and her bloodhound would sneak off in search of new golden objects.

Nancy would release Sniffer and he would follow the scent of gold.

Sniffer always returned with something shiny and valuable, which Nancy put in her sack.

Nancy would carry the new treasures home to her cottage. Her cupboards were crammed with golden goodies.

There were golden necklaces, golden candlesticks, golden goblets, golden plates, golden teapots, golden coins, golden rings, golden earrings, golden bracelets, golden brooches, golden trinkets, golden thimbles, and even a golden dog bowl!

Chapter Two

Now one day in the land of Trittledore, the old king died. His handsome son was declared the new king.

A new crown was made for the occasion. It was studded with the finest jewels and made with the shiniest gold.

There were celebrations throughout the land and everyone admired the new king's splendid treasure.

People could not stop talking about his beautiful new crown, so word spread throughout the land.

It was not long before Naughty Nancy also heard the news about the king's priceless crown. She became jealous. "I'm going to make that crown my own," she said.

Chapter Three

Naughty Nancy found an old map of the castle and placed it under Sniffer's nose to show him where they were going.

Sniffer gave it several deep sniffs then wagged his tail. Then they waited for night to come.

When the sky had turned black they crept to the edge of the woods where they could see the king's castle. Sniffer caught the scent of gold in his nostrils.

Sniffer crept up to the castle and dived into the moat.

He doggy-paddled carefully across the water.

Then he climbed up the bank on the other side.

He spied an open window and scrambled inside the castle.

Sniffer followed the scent of gold.
His muddy paws took him up a flight
of steps.

He went along
a corridor, past
the royal
bathroom and
into the king's
bedroom itself...

He carefully picked the crown up in
his mouth and crept out of the room.

Sniffer scampered past some sleeping guards then doggy-paddled back across the moat again.

Naughty Nancy was waiting for him at the edge of the forest. She clapped her hands in glee when she saw the golden crown in Sniffer's jaws.

She placed it firmly on her head and jumped for joy.
The crown really was hers!
Her naughty plan had worked.
So Naughty Nancy danced all the way home.

Chapter Four

The next morning, Naughty Nancy awoke with the crown still on her head. She admired herself in the mirror. "It's so beautiful!" she sighed.

"Now I just need to brush my hair to show off its beauty even more."

Nancy grasped the crown and tried to remove it, but she couldn't. It was stuck. She tugged and tugged, then tugged again even harder, but it just would not budge. "Fiddlesticks!" she said.

"I need your help, Sniffer," said Nancy.
Sniffer held the crown in his jaws and
pulled hard. But he could not get it off.

"Goosepimples," Nancy muttered.
"What can I try next?"

Nancy wedged the crown in the door and pulled with all her strength. She turned this way and that way but still it would not come off.

Just then Sniffer started barking loudly. "What's the matter?" Nancy asked.

Naughty Nancy peered through the window to see if anyone was outside. To her horror she saw the king's soldiers. They were heading towards the cottage.

Chapter Five

Nancy grabbed a towel and wrapped it around her head. She wanted to hide the stolen crown.

Suddenly there was a loud knock at the door.

Nancy nervously opened the door.

A big soldier stood before her.

"The king's crown has been stolen!"

he snapped.

Nancy's knees started knocking.

"We followed some muddy paw prints from the king's bedroom which led us to your house," he added. Nancy's knees knocked even more.

Then the soldier spotted all the golden objects in Nancy's cottage. "What a lot of gold you have," he observed.

Sniffer started to snivel.

Then the soldier spied Nancy's bloodhound. "And what a big nose for a dog!"

Sniffer snivelled even more.

The soldier looked suspicious. "Do you happen to know where the crown is?" he demanded.

Naughty Nancy felt scared and wasn't sure how to reply.

She shook her head repeatedly…

…but as she did so…

…the towel slipped from her head.

"Aha!" cried the soldier as the crown was revealed. "There it is!"

And so he arrested Nancy and Sniffer on the spot. Nancy knew there was no escape.

Chapter Six

Naughty Nancy and Sniffer were taken to the castle and were brought before the king. Nancy hung her head low in shame.

The handsome king arose from his throne and stepped towards Nancy.

"Ah, my most precious treasure!" the king sighed. "How lovely, how wonderful, how beautiful!"

But the king was not talking about his crown, he was talking about Nancy.

"I have found my lost treasure," he announced, "and she who wears it I desire even more. Please will you marry me?"

Nancy didn't need to be asked twice. She nodded her head to accept his proposal. She liked the idea of getting married to someone so handsome and regal.

So Naughty Nancy stopped being naughty. She realized what a bad person she had been. She was truly sorry and returned all her stolen things. But the magnificent crown was forever stuck on her head.

The king had a new crown made for himself that matched Naughty Nancy's. And they lived together happily ever after.

And as for Sniffer... well, he got a job guarding the crown jewels!

About the Author and Illustrator

Roger Abbott lives in Leicestershire and has been writing short stories since his teens. He came up with the idea for *Sniffer and Naughty Nancy* many years ago. Roger says, "As a child I was always reading and developed a vivid imagination. If Sniffer was my pet dog I'd certainly be tempted to put his special talent to good use!"

Colin West has been writing and illustrating books for children for as long as he can remember. He works in the attic studio of his house in Epping which he shares with his wife Cathie. He loves capturing the right expressions in his drawings of people and had special fun doing the same for Sniffer. Colin says, "I used up nearly all my yellow paint depicting the golden objects in this story!"

Tips for Beginner Readers

1. Think about the cover and the title of the book. What do you think it will be about? While you are reading, think about what might happen next and why.

2. As you read, ask yourself if what you're reading makes sense. If it doesn't, try rereading or look at the pictures for clues.

3. If there is a word that you do not know, look carefully at the letters, sounds, and word parts that you do know. Blend the sounds to read the word. Is this a word you know? Does it make sense in the sentence?

4. Think about the characters, where the story takes place, and the problems the characters in the story faced. What are the important ideas in the beginning, middle and end of the story?

5. Ask yourself questions like:
Did you like the story?
Why or why not?
How did the author make it fun to read?
How well did you understand it?

Maybe you can understand the story better if you read it again!